SHREDDER
THE SPIDER DROID

With special thanks to Brandon Robshaw

ORCHARD BOOKS
338 Euston Road, London NW1 3BH
Orchard Books Australia
Level 17/207 Kent St, Sydney, NSW 2000

A Paperback Original
First published in Great Britain in 2013

Sea Quest is a registered trademark of Beast Quest Limited
Series created by Beast Quest Limited, London

Text © Beast Quest Limited 2013
Cover and inside illustrations by Artful Doodlers,
with special thanks to Bob and Justin © Orchard Books 2013

A CIP catalogue record for this book is available from
the British Library.

ISBN 978 1 40832 411 0

1 3 5 7 9 10 8 6 4 2

Printed and bound by CPI Group (UK) Ltd, Croydon, CR0 4YY

The paper and board used in this paperback are natural recyclable
products made from wood grown in sustainable forests. The
manufacturing processes conform to the environmental regulations of
the country of origin.

Orchard Books is a division of Hachette Children's Books,
an Hachette UK company

www.hachette.co.uk

SHREDDER
THE SPIDER DROID

BY ADAM BLADE

ORCHARD

SPECTRON, 3,548 FATHOMS DEEP,
THE CAVERN OF GHOSTS

I've done it! At last I perfected my new invention. When the Professor strikes, I believe it could foil his evil plan…

Now I must find him. Someone has to stop him, and nobody knows him as well as I do. It will be hard to leave the Sea Ghosts unprotected. They are so kind and innocent, and have shared everything with me, all of their carefully collected treasures of the sea. I fear that they have even come to think of me as their guardian.

But I must leave if their world is to be saved. I can only hope that my new device will be enough to stop the Professor.

If it isn't, the Cavern of Ghosts – and everything that lies above – is doomed…

>LOG ENTRY ENDS

CHAPTER ONE

THE SEA GHOST

"Ready, Riv?" asked Max.

He held out the rocketball. Rivet eyed it and rose up on his hind legs. The dogbot's metal tongue hung out and his electronic voicebox made panting sounds.

Max grinned. Rivet loved playing fetch. But it was impossible to throw a normal ball any distance underwater. That's why Max had designed and built the jet-propelled rocketball.

He drew back his arm, and threw the

ball. It zoomed across the ocean floor, leaving two jet-trails behind it. Rivet gave an electronic bark and shot after it, leaving a trail of bubbles and changing course as the rocketball bounced off rocks and clumps of seaweed.

It felt like the old days on the island city of Aquora, when Max used to throw a normal ball for Rivet. Max's father, Callum, had returned to Aquora just two weeks ago, after Max had rescued him from the clutches of his uncle, the evil Professor. Max shivered at the thought of his uncle – a power-mad scientific genius who was trying to become the ruler of the whole ocean.

Max had chosen to remain here, in the undersea city of Sumara. He missed his father, but the Professor had hinted that his long-lost mother was alive and under the waves somewhere. Max's father didn't believe the

Professor's words, but Max was determined to find his mother if it was the last thing he did. The undersea world was full of secrets, and he felt sure that his uncle knew more about his mother's disappearance than he had admitted.

In fact, Max would have liked to set out on a Quest to look for her right away. But without any clues to guide him, it was impossible to know where to start. The ocean was so vast.

Rivet swam back towards him, the rocketball clamped in his jaws. His stumpy metal tail wagged, and he looked as if he was smiling.

"Again, Max!" he barked, letting the ball float free. "Again!"

Max took the ball and held it high. "Ready?"

"Hey, Max!" a new voice said. "What have you got there?"

Max turned and saw his best friend, Lia.

She wore a green tunic of plaited seaweed, and her long silver hair billowed in the water. Her pet swordfish, Spike, swam beside her. Lia was a Princess of the underwater people called Merryn, and it was she who had given Max the power to breathe below the waves.

"I call it a rocketball," Max said. "I just finished making it this morning. Look, it's jet-propelled—"

"Jet-propelled?" Lia said. The Merryn had little understanding of technology.

"Sort of like a squid," Max explained. "It pushes out water behind it so it can travel fast through the water."

Lia frowned. "Can I have a go?"

"Sure." Max handed her the ball. "Careful, though. You don't need to throw it hard because—"

Too late. Lia had already hurled the rocketball with all her strength.

The ball went hurtling through the water. Rivet gave chase, but the rocketball streaked into the gloom of the ocean and was soon lost to sight.

"Oops!" Lia said. "Sorry, Max."

"It doesn't matter," Max said. But he really

hoped the ball wasn't lost – he had spent all day making it. "Let's see if we can find it."

They swam together in the direction the ball had gone. Ahead, Rivet was sniffing around among the rocks and coral, hunting for the rocketball. A shoal of fish rose from a patch of kelp, disturbed by Rivet's snuffling, and darted away.

Max, Lia and Spike joined in the search. But there was no sign of the ball.

They came to a large outcrop of rocks. "It could have gone in one of the gaps between the rocks," Max said. "And if it did, we'll never find it."

Is this what you're looking for? said a voice in Max's head. He started, his skin prickling at the strange feeling of hearing someone speak inside his skull. He looked up and saw a figure rising from behind the rocks. He caught his breath.

It was a boy, about Max's own age – but unlike any boy he had ever seen. He was almost transparent. Max could just see the faint, milky outline of his body. If the boy had bones, they were transparent too. A seahorse swam behind him and Max could still see its shape through him. The only solid-looking parts of the boy were the vivid green orbs of his eyes.

Max turned to Lia. "What is it?" he whispered in amazement.

She just stared at the boy, her eyes wide with alarm. Spike was slowly rotating his fins and edging backwards. Rivet stood his ground, feet planted, and gave a defiant bark.

The ghostly boy held the rocketball in his pale hand.

Here you go.

There it was again – the voice in Max's head. The ghostly boy's lips hadn't moved. He was talking to Max telepathically.

"Did you hear that?" Max said to Lia.

"I didn't hear anything," Lia said in a tense voice. "Come on, let's go." She tugged anxiously at Max's arm.

"Why, what's the matter?" Max asked.

"It's...a Sea Ghost," Lia said.

"A ghost? You mean he's dead?"

"Of course not, don't be silly. They're not dead, just...dangerous. I've never seen one before, but my dad used to tell me stories about them. All the legends say they bring bad luck."

It's not true, said the voice in Max's head. *Please, don't listen to her. My people need your help.*

CHAPTER TWO

"MY ENEMY'S ENEMY"

"What are you waiting for?" Lia said, tugging at Max's arm.

Spike had already retreated some distance away, where he was swimming in impatient circles. Rivet was staring at the strange floating boy, as if trying to work out what he was.

"Wait," Max said. "He said he needs help, so we should at least find out—"

We do need your help. Please.

There it was again. "You must have heard that," Max said to Lia.

"Heard what?"

Max spoke to the boy. "My friend can't hear what you're saying to me. Do you speak Merryn?"

The boy's mouth opened, and a thin, quiet voice came out. "A little."

"What's your name?"

"My name Ko."

The boy seemed less strange now he had a name, Max thought. More of a person. "Hello, Ko. My name's—"

"Your name Max."

Max was amazed. Was the Sea Ghost reading his mind?

The boy pointed a pale, translucent finger at Max's friend. "And this Lia."

Lia looked shocked and not very pleased. "How did you know that?" she demanded.

"Even my people, far from here, know of you. You heroes, you fight monsterbeasts. Many stories. My people in danger, my people need you."

"In danger?" Max said. He didn't want to refuse the boy's plea for help. "How?"

"Bad man attack our city. Powerful man. He has deadly...machines to fight for him." He pointed at Rivet. Rivet trotted closer to him, wagging his tail. "Like this, but very big. And bad. My people not know machines. You help? Please?"

Max's heartbeat quickened. A bad man with deadly machines? It had to be the Professor! This was his chance to seek him out. The last time Max saw him, the Professor had said that he knew where Max's mother was. This could be the clue he needed to find her...

He turned to Lia. "We have to help."

Lia frowned. "Why can't his people help

themselves?" she muttered.

Max wondered how to persuade her. *But I guess she can't help distrusting Sea Ghosts*, he thought. *She's heard so many bad stories about them.*

It is not her fault, the voice in his mind said.

"I know it's not her fault!" Max said.

"Who are you speaking to?" Lia asked. "What's happening?"

"He's speaking to me, inside my mind," Max said. "Telepathy."

Lia's eyes narrowed, and she frowned at Ko. "They are a strange people. Not like us."

"We still have to help them. You know what the Professor's like – he nearly destroyed Sumara. Now he's at it again!"

Lia didn't answer for a short while. Her lower lip stuck out as she thought. "All right," she said eventually. "I suppose my enemy's enemy is my friend. Well, not *friend* exactly."

Max heaved a sigh of relief. He wasn't sure how he would have managed to help Ko without Lia. They had been through so many adventures together, they were a team now. "Let's go back to Sumara and get my aquabike," he said. "Then we'll follow Ko!"

Rivet barked excitedly. "Quest, Max?"

"Yes, Riv," Max said. "Another Quest."

"Fine, but the Sea Ghost must wait here," Lia said. "If he comes to Sumara, he'll bring bad luck to the entire city."

"Of course he won't!" Max said.

"He'll scare everyone," Lia said.

"Don't leave me here," Ko said. He drifted closer to them. "If you go without me, you not come back!"

Lia looked at him angrily. "Of course we'll come back. I don't know about your people, but we Merryn keep our word!"

"Oh, let him come with us," Max said.

"What harm can it do?"

Rivet barked as if in agreement.

Lia gave a snort, but stopped arguing.

They headed back to the city. Lia took the lead, rushing ahead as if she wanted to get this over with. Spike swam beside her. But Ko was fast too. He swam with an unusual motion, not moving his arms and legs so

much as rippling his whole boneless body, like an eel, easily keeping pace with Lia. Max and Rivet brought up the rear. Max's swimming had improved a lot since he'd lived under the sea, but he still couldn't swim as fast as those who'd been born here.

Soon Max saw the gleaming lights of Sumara up ahead. The city was built in an undersea valley. It was a great sprawl of dwellings carved from different-coloured rock, lit by shining yellow lamp-globes. In the centre, the tall pink towers of the King's coral palace soared proudly above the houses.

Just outside the city, they passed a Merryn farmer leading a herd of grouper fish out to pasture. When he saw Ko his mouth opened in horror and he hastily led his fish in the other direction. Max and Lia exchanged a glance.

As they entered the city, Merryn people

shrank away from them, muttering. The streets emptied as Ko approached.

Everyone's frightened of Sea Ghosts, Max realised.

The weirdest thing was the effect Ko had on the lamp-globes that lit the city. They were filled with a glowing substance, taken from deep-sea angler fish – but as Ko went

by, their glow dimmed almost to blackness. Then the light came back after he had passed.

Maybe there is something to those old stories, Max thought. *Maybe Sea Ghosts do bring bad luck...*

CHAPTER THREE

A SECRET TUNNEL

"All right," Max said. "You can come out now, Ko."

The giant clamshell that the Merryn had given Max for a home opened up a fraction. Ko squeezed through the gap, his body almost flattened. Once outside he resumed his normal shape.

It had been Lia's idea for Ko to hide until they'd visited the palace to say goodbye to her father. King Salinus would never have let them go on a journey with a Sea Ghost.

Max sat astride the gleaming aquabike his father had fixed up. His fingers tapped the handlebars impatiently – he was eager to be gone, excited at the thought of another Quest. The storage compartment was loaded with food, tools and a medical kit. Max revved the engine.

Ko started at the noise and his big green eyes goggled at the aquabike. "What this machine do?"

"It's for travelling fast through the water," Max said. "Jump on, you'll see."

Ko slid onto the seat behind Max. His hand briefly touched Max's arm. The Sea Ghost's skin felt cool and jelly-like, but surprisingly firm.

"Everyone will stare at us if we travel through Sumara with him sitting on the back," Lia said. "I hope no one tells my father."

"Oh, you are leaving Sumara?" said a voice. Max and Lia spun round to see Tarla, who had swum up behind them. She wore the blue robe that showed she was one of the Merryn healers. Her wise, wrinkled face was kindly but serious. She raised an eyebrow at

Ko. "And you are going with the Sea Ghost?"

"It was Max's idea," Lia said.

"Sea Ghosts are creatures of bad luck," Tarla said. "So the legends say."

"That is myth," Ko said.

Tarla looked thoughtfully into Ko's face. He blinked at her.

"I have never seen a Sea Ghost before," Tarla said. "You are as strange as the legends report."

"To me, you are the strange ones," Ko said. Tarla chuckled at that.

"He needs our help!" Max said. "His people are under attack from the Professor."

"What do you think, Tarla?" Lia asked. "Can we trust him?"

"The legends say not," Tarla said. "And often, the legends speak true. But...not always. If you are set on this Quest—"

"We are!" Max said.

"Then you must carry it through. I admire your bravery. But remember the power of the Pearls of Honour."

Tarla pointed at the glittering silver clasp pinned to Max's suit. Max reached up to touch the pearls embedded in it. Lia's father had given one to him and one to Lia after they had completed their first Quest by finding the four parts of the Skull of Thallos. The Pearls of Honour were filled with ancient Aqua Powers and could summon the help of any sea creatures nearby. Knowing that they had the Pearls of Honour made Max feel a little better.

"And you won't tell my father where we're going?" Lia asked Tarla.

Tarla shook her head. "But the Sea Ghost needs a disguise – or he will attract attention." She took a coral box from the pocket of her robe, and smeared some ointment on Ko's forehead. His milky outline faded away until he was invisible. Even his eyes were no more than a pale green glimmer.

"Wow!" Max gasped. "What is that stuff?"

"Extract of Cloakweed," Tarla said.

"What you do to me?" Ko asked.

"It won't hurt you," Tarla said. "The effect only lasts a short while. You will soon be visible again."

"Then we'd better be going!" Lia said.

Max nodded. "Thanks, Tarla." He twisted the throttle. "Jump on, Rivet." The dogbot scrambled onto the pannier beside Ko.

They roared out of the city, Lia and Spike swimming alongside. *Goodbye, Sumara,* Max thought. *I hope we'll see you again.*

When Sumara was no more than a distant glow behind them, Max eased off the throttle and the aquabike drifted to a halt. Ko slipped off the back. His milky outline could be seen again, and his eyes glowed green.

"So, which way now?" Lia asked.

"Follow me," said Ko.

He turned and swam away with startling speed, in his strange, pulsing style. Max, Lia, Spike and Rivet followed. But Ko had hardly gone any distance when he stopped, floating above a luxuriant carpet of kelp that grew on the ocean floor. It was green, brown, orange,

yellow and gold, and tiny, brightly coloured fish swam among the waving fronds. "Here."

"Here?" Lia said disbelievingly. "So close to Sumara? Is this a joke?"

"Is not joke." Ko swam to the middle of the seaweed patch and rummaged around. He tugged aside several large fronds of seaweed.

Max eased the bike over to where Ko was. Lia and Spike followed.

Beneath the seaweed was a gaping hole, the entrance to a rocky tunnel that led down into darkness.

"This way," Ko said, pointing with his pale hand. Before Max could ask any questions, Ko dived headfirst into the tunnel.

Max peered over the edge. He could see Ko, swimming further and further away. In the darkness his body glowed pale green.

"I guess we follow," Max said.

"Are you sure?" Lia asked. "We have no

idea what's down there."

You must follow! said Ko's voice in Max's head. *Think of your mother.*

"How do you know about my mum?" Max said aloud.

Your story is well known among my people, said Ko's voice. *I told you that.*

Max turned to Lia. "Following Ko will lead

us to the Professor – which may lead me to my mother. And besides – we said we'd help, didn't we? We can't go back on that."

Lia nodded, slowly. Spike looked at her anxiously, and she patted his head. "Don't worry – it'll be all right. Probably."

"Come on, Rivet!" Max said. His dogbot's tail wagged. Max took a deep breath and rode the aquabike straight down into the mouth of the tunnel. Immediately he felt a current pulling him downwards. Rivet swam alongside him, his propellers churning.

"It's dark," Lia's voice said close behind him.

It was more than dark. It was pitch black. Max switched on the aquabike's lights and the golden beam picked out the pale green shape of Ko below.

I just hope we're doing the right thing, he thought.

As they travelled further down, Max

noticed twinkling crystals lining the walls of the tunnel. They were of every colour – red, green, purple, rose, amber – and there were more and more the further Max descended. He felt like he was inside a kaleidoscope.

The deeper they got, the more the water pressed in on them. Soon Max found it hard to breathe. It felt as if an iron weight lay on his chest. He had heard stories of how, at very great depths, the pressure was enough to crush a person – perhaps even a human like himself who had been given the Merryn Touch, so that he could breathe underwater. A cold dread gripped him. He had never been this deep before.

"Max!" Rivet said. "Water squashing me."

"Me too," Max managed to say.

"I'm scared," Rivet said.

"Me too," Max said again. It was an effort to get the words out.

Lia and Spike swam up beside them. Lia was struggling for breath, and Spike's eyes bulged in distress.

"We have to go back!" Lia said. "The pressure is too great."

Max didn't know how much more he could stand – but he hated the thought of giving up already.

Up ahead, the glowing green shape of Ko came to a halt. "Is all right!" called the Sea Ghost. "We arrive!"

As Max's aquabike drew level with Ko, the headlights shone onto a wall of black rock ahead.

"So now what?" Lia panted.

"We go through!" Ko said. He pointed to a narrow slit in the rock. It was just about big enough for Max to get a hand through.

"How are we supposed to get through that?" Lia demanded.

"I squeeze," Ko explained. "You must break rock."

Ko pushed himself into the gap. His flexible body flattened as he squeezed through. A moment later he had disappeared from view.

"Now you break rock!" he called, from the other side. "Make hole big."

"What with?" Lia said. "Our bare hands?"

Despite the pressure on his chest, Max

managed a grin. "Don't worry. I picked up some aquamines from the Graveyard near Sumara. Now's the time to use them."

The Graveyard was where the Merryn people kept tools and weapons lost by Aquoran sailors. They did not understand technology and had no use for it themselves, but Max had found lots of useful items there.

He dug in the aquabike's pannier and took out three aquamines. They were red metal, shaped like starfish, and filled with high explosive. He wedged them into the gap.

"Get ready," he said. "They'll blow after a count of ten!"

He switched on the aquamines and quickly pushed away from the rock.

"Everybody back!" he shouted. "As far as you can!"

Max, Lia, Spike and Rivet scrambled up the tunnel as fast as they could.

"Five," Max whispered. "Four. Three. Two. One…"

CHAPTER FOUR

THE CRYSTAL COLUMN

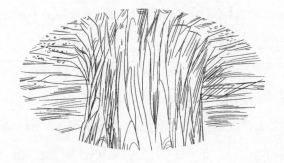

Whooomph!

The explosion made a muffled, heavy sound. Max felt the beat of it in his eardrums, and a moment later a powerful current rushed up the tunnel. It hurled him, Lia, Spike and Rivet upwards. Max was flung from the saddle of his aquabike, but he managed to hang onto the handlebars.

"What's happening?" screamed Lia.

"Maybe three aquamines was too many!"

Max shouted back.

At last the wave subsided. As the water fell, they sank with it. Now Max felt the current seize him like a giant hand and tug him downwards. They were being sucked towards the gap, like leaves going down a drain.

If the mines haven't made a big enough hole, we'll be smashed against the rock, Max realised.

All he could see was a torrent of foaming black water, with the golden beam of the headlamps swinging wildly through it.

Then he caught a glimpse of a huge jagged hole rushing towards them, like a mouth with splintered teeth. The aquabike smashed into the side as they were yanked through. It spun round and was wrenched from Max's grip.

He caught a glimpse of Lia being whirled along beside him, her face pale and scared.

Max felt his stomach lurch, as if he'd suddenly become weightless. The current wasn't pulling them now. They were falling.

Plummeting!

Max's head broke through the water. He let out a cry and gulped in a lungful of air.

In an instant, his eyes took in the scene. They were tumbling down a gigantic waterfall towards a huge expanse of gleaming water.

Max saw Lia beside him, turning and twisting as she fell. Her head was out of the water and her mouth gaped helplessly. *Of course!* She couldn't breathe air like a human.

"Hold on, Lia!" Max yelled, above the roar of the waterfall. "We're nearly—"

The sea rushed up to meet them.

SPLASH!

They hit the surface with an almighty smack, and the air was knocked out of Max's lungs. He was pulled under the water by a spiralling current, broke free and bobbed up again, gasping as his head broke the surface.

Rivet's head popped up beside him, water streaming off his snout.

"Are you all right, Riv?"

"Ouch, Max!"

Max looked around in wonder. They were in a vast cavern – so vast he could not see where it ended. High above was a domed roof of rock, twinkling with crystals like the ones Max had seen in the tunnel. The waterfall cascaded from a split about halfway up the wall, creating a creamy whirlpool where it hit the underground sea.

Ko appeared beside them, his head poking above the water. Like Max he seemed to have no trouble breathing air. Under the surface he was gripping the handlebars of Max's aquabike. "I found your machine, Max."

"Thanks," Max said. "But – what happened?"

"Your explosion break wall. Make waterfall."

"What is this place?"

"Hydrophantia," Ko said with a touch of pride. "My people live here. Some call it the Cavern of Ghosts."

We made it, Max thought. *But where's Lia?*

He took the bike from Ko, gunned the engine into life and dived beneath the sea. Rivet barked and dived with him.

As his eyes adjusted, Max saw Lia and Spike

swimming over. Lia looked relieved to be back in her element. "Where are we?" she asked.

"In some kind of underground world. It's amazing! You have to see it."

"How can I? I can't breathe up there."

Max reached into the storage compartment of the aquabike and took out an Amphibio mask. Its special filter allowed the wearer to breathe oxygen, whether in water or air. "Here, put this on."

Lia looked a little reluctant. But she strapped the mask on, and she and Spike swam to the surface with Max and Rivet.

Ko was waiting there for them. "Welcome to my world," he said with a ghostly grin.

"You've got a funny way of welcoming people," Lia said. She gazed around her. "It's big," was all she said.

In the distance, Max saw a tall, glittering column rising from the water. It was immensely thick, and reached all the way up to the cavern roof.

"What's that?" he asked Ko.

"Crystal Column," Ko answered. "No one knows who made it. Legends say it holds up sky."

Maybe those legends are right, Max thought. He imagined the column being suddenly removed – would that immense rocky roof collapse under its own weight?

Max looked at the Crystal Column, calculating the distance and direction. It was hard to be sure, but...

"What do you think's above that?" he asked.

Lia looked blank for a moment, then her eyes went wide. "We must be just underneath Sumara!"

"If anything happened to that column," Max said, "Sumara would come crashing down into Hydrophantia. The city would be utterly

ruined." The thought made his stomach squirm. "The Professor's always wanted to wreck Sumara so he can rule the ocean, and now he might destroy Hydrophantia too!"

Lia looked alarmed. "I bet that's what he's

planning. We have to stop him! It's a good thing we came to help." She turned to Ko. "Sorry I didn't trust you at first."

"That not matter," Ko said politely.

"So what do we do now?" Max asked.

"We wait," Ko said. "People come to meet us here."

"What people?" Max asked.

Before Ko could reply, Rivet barked. "Noise, Max!"

Max strained to listen. At once he heard the noise too. A distant droning, getting louder and louder...

"They are coming," Ko said.

Max spun round to see strange shapes hovering above the sea and coming towards them. Six of them. Long, spindly metal creatures with whirring wings, tentacles that ended in pincers, and blank steel faces.

Attack Bots!

CHAPTER FIVE

TRAPPED!

"We have to get out of here!" Max shouted.

The Attack Bots droned louder and louder, swooping down on them. Lia dived. Max tilted the aquabike and plunged beneath the water to join her.

Lia was swimming fast. "If we dive deep maybe we can lose them!" she called back.

Max followed her down into the depths, with Ko, Spike and Rivet keeping pace.

There was a huge splash from above as the

Attack Bots hit the water like rockets. Max saw the trail of bubbles each one left as it zoomed down to their level. With incredible speed, they formed a circle round Max and the others. They had folded their wings in and extended their tentacles. They looked rather like robotic squid, but eyeless.

The largest Attack Bot spoke, its voice booming through the water.

"Hello again, Max! Outwitting you is too

easy – can't you try a bit harder?"

Max's heart sank. The Attack Bot had his uncle's voice. He must be controlling it from a distance. "It's the Professor," Max said to Ko. "How did he know to find us here?"

"How do you think?" Lia said. "The Sea Ghost set this up!"

Max looked at Ko. The Sea Ghost's shoulders sagged, and he did not meet Max's eyes.

I'm sorry, said the voice in Max's head.

"I told you we couldn't trust him!" Lia said bitterly.

"I not have choice," Ko said in his halting Merryn. His green eyes were pleading. "Professor take my mother. Put her in prison. Say he not let her free if I not help him."

"Clever plan, wasn't it?" the Professor's voice said. "I knew you'd fall for it, Max – you can never resist being a little do-gooder!"

At first Max felt furious with Ko. He would

have liked to shout at him, tell him what a double-crossing sea snake he was. But when he thought about it...could he blame Ko? After all, the Sea Ghost was only protecting his mother. Wouldn't Max do the same?

"You'd better go, then," he said to Ko. "You've done your job."

I'm truly sorry, the voice in Max's head said. *I was given no choice.*

Ko turned and swam away, aiming for a gap between the nearest Attack Bots. Instantly, the closest one shot out its steel pincers and gripped Ko around the middle, jerking him away and making him squeal in alarm.

The Professor's laugh boomed out. "Did you really think I'd let you go? First lesson in life: trust no one! Now you've served your purpose, you can join dear Mummy in prison."

"What do you want with us?" Max shouted.

"You and your little Merryn friend have

been a thorn in my side for too long," the Professor said. "I'm going to ask you one last time, Max: join me. You're young and naive, but you're smart and you have plenty of spirit. I could do with you on my team, and you'd learn a lot from me – perhaps even find what you're searching for..."

"No," Max said. "I'll never join you!"

He reached for the clasp pinned to his tunic and touched the Pearls of Honour. Any minute now, sea creatures would come to their aid... But nothing happened. He looked at Lia, and she shrugged.

"Oh dear," chuckled the Professor. "It seems your Merryn tricks don't work down here in the Cavern of Ghosts. No one's coming to save you, Max. So you can join Ko and his mother in prison. And so can the Merryn girl and that stupid fat fish of hers. On second thoughts, I'll probably eat the fish. Roasted, and stuffed with shrimps. Delicious."

Lia's mouth fell open in horror. Spike moved close to her and she put her arm around him protectively.

"We'll fight our way out," Max said softly. "Ready?"

She nodded.

Quickly Max pulled out the hyperblade from the aquabike's storage compartment. It was a thin, curved blade of solid vernium, the hardest substance known on Nemos. Then he twisted the throttle and drove the aquabike straight at the Attack Bot with the Professor's voice. Rivet shot forward beside him.

Lia yelled out a war cry as she and Spike darted towards the one next to it.

The lead Attack Bot easily fended Max off with its steel tentacles. Rivet clanged into the robot, knocking it backwards.

Max swung the aquabike around and came

in from the side. He struck at the Attack Bot's head with his hyperblade, but the robot's tentacle parried the blow. It tried to grab Max with another tentacle, but he ducked. Max struck again and this time the hyperblade bit into the Attack Bot's outer casing, releasing a shower of sparks. Before he could do any more, he felt steel tentacles tighten around his middle, gripping so tight he could hardly breathe. Another Attack Bot had grabbed him from behind! He was pulled off the aquabike, which tumbled down towards the ocean floor. *The last thing my father gave me*, he thought sadly as the aquabike disappeared from view.

Rivet attacked again, seizing the second Attack Bot's tentacle in his jaws. But the first one grabbed the dogbot and tucked him under its arm. Rivet twisted and barked but couldn't break free.

Max struggled, but the Attack Bot held him

fast. He saw Lia and Spike fighting valiantly against another of the Professor's creatures. Spike thrust at the robot with his sword-like bill, driving it backwards. But two more Bots came to help. One grabbed Lia, and the other snatched up Spike.

"That was fun!" the Professor said. "I like a good fight, as long as the odds are stacked in my favour!"

His Attack Bot extended its tentacles and lifted Max over its head, pressing him against its back. It pressed a button on a control panel, and suddenly a transparent bubble ballooned out from its body, trapping Max inside. Max pushed and kicked against the bubble. It was stretchy and yielding, but super-tough. He tried cutting it with his hyperblade, but the surface simply bulged out where the blade pressed.

"Nice try," the Professor said. "It's a material

of my own invention. Hyperblade-proof, so don't waste your time. Now, off to prison you must go!"

Max looked around and saw all his friends – Lia, Ko, Rivet and Spike – each trapped in their own bubble and struggling to escape. But it was no good. The Attack Bots zoomed through the water in a V formation, with Max and the Professor's Attack Bot at the head.

There was nothing Max could do but watch the world of Hydrophantia gliding by. The sea creatures here were different from those in the upper oceans of Nemos. He saw pale fish with drooping whiskers and enormous eyes, a writhing creature that seemed to have about a hundred legs, and a curious, pulsing thing that looked like a giant blob of jelly. Each creature glimmered, half see-through, with its own eerie light.

They were heading towards the Crystal Column. As they came closer, Max realised that it was even bigger than it had looked from a distance. Soon it filled his whole field of vision. He felt reassured by one thing at least – if the Professor was planning to destroy this gigantic column, it wouldn't be easy.

The Attack Bots came to a stop by the underside of some sort of contraption floating next to the Crystal Column. It looked to Max like an immense spider's web in a cube shape, made from strands of glowing silver material.

The Attack Bots' wings unfurled and they rose up out of the water. Now Max saw that inside the web was a metal building with rows of cells, connected by walkways. This must be the prison the Professor had spoken of!

Max's gaze travelled upwards, and he gasped in disbelief.

On top of the web that surrounded the prison sat an enormous robotic spider. It had a round metal body, and its skull-like head held eight glowing red electronic eyes. Its giant legs gripped the sides of the spider's-web cage. It looked down at the new arrivals and its jaws opened and shut hungrily.

"I see you're admiring my creation," the Professor's voice said. "I call him Shredder. Isn't he a beauty?"

The Attack Bots moved in closer to the

cage. Shredder lifted its eight giant legs, and there was a buzzing sound. The network of shining silver strands suddenly disappeared, leaving only the inner structure of chambers surrounded by walkways.

Max's Attack Bot flew into the prison, landing on a metal walkway. The bubble holding Max opened in one smooth movement and he slid onto the floor. Lia and Ko soon came tumbling down next to Max. The Attack Bots carrying Spike and Rivet flew further into the prison system, and were soon lost from sight.

The giant spider's legs lowered above them. There was another buzz and the web of shining struts sprang into place again, locking them in.

"So here we are!" The Professor's voice boomed from speakers mounted along the walkways. "Welcome to my floating prison. Impressive, isn't it? I hope you'll be comfortable here. I'm only sorry I can't join you in person – but I'll be with you soon, and when I arrive I'll eat that fine fat fish! Don't try and escape, by the way. The outer bars are beams of pure energy and they'd burn your hands off. Even if you got past those, you'd still have Shredder to reckon with – and frankly, I wouldn't fancy your chances!"

CHAPTER SIX

JOLLY ROGER

Six robots came scuttling along the walkway. Each one walked on eight spindly legs and had glowing red eyes – smaller versions of the giant spider sitting atop the prison.

"Don't move!" commanded the front Spider Bot. Its voice was harsh and metallic. "You will now be searched."

The Spider Bot rose up on four of its legs and used the other four to frisk Max. It quickly pulled the hyperblade from his belt and stored it in a compartment in its body. *Oh no!* Max thought. With the hyperblade he might have had a chance of cutting through the prison bars.

Next the Spider Bot found the rocketball. It stared at Max's invention, clicking and whirring. Max guessed that its computer-brain was trying to work out what it was.

"No known weapon type," it finally announced. "Object identified as harmless."

The Spider Bot returned the rocketball to Max, who tucked it away in his suit.

Two other Spider Bots searched Lia and Ko, and, finding nothing, lowered themselves back onto eight legs.

"Search completed," the Spider Bot that had searched Max announced. He seemed to be the leader. "Escort prisoners to Cell 328."

Two of the Spider Bots got behind Max, Lia and Ko. Two more marched on either side.

The other two led the way into the prison, their metal legs scrabbling on the walkway. There was no way for Max and his friends to escape.

Max peered into the cells as they passed. They were barred with closely woven struts of metal, but through the chinks he could catch brief glimpses of the occupants. Some were Sea Ghosts, pale and forlorn. In one cell he saw two of the green, scaly Kroy people, whom Max and Lia had met on their quest to defeat Manak the Silent Predator. Some cells had glass walls and were filled with water – they contained Merryn people. And other cells held strange humanoid creatures Max had never seen before – beings with horns and fins and tentacles, shrouded in gloom.

"Looks like the Professor's been busy," Max said. "He must have captured just about every kind of creature on Nemos!"

"Yes, and now we're joining them," Lia said.

"I am very sorry," Ko said, hanging his head.

Lia glared at him. "I bet you are," she said. "This is what you get for making deals with the Professor."

"Silence!" the leader of the Spider Bots rapped out. "No talking among the prisoners."

They tramped on, turning several corners and going down a flight of iron steps. At last the Spider Bots came to a halt outside a cell with the number 328 flickering on a screen above it.

The Spider Bot extended one of its limbs and a key card flicked out. It inserted the card into a slot, and a section of the criss-crossed bars slid open.

"Prisoners, enter!" the Spider Bot said.

Max felt a metal limb pushing him into the cell from behind. Lia and Ko were pushed in next. The door clanged shut, and the Spider

Bots scurried away. They were alone.

"Welcome, cellmates," said a deep voice from a dark corner of the cell.

Max spun round. A man was leaning against the wall. He was tall, with a craggy face, an eye patch and long hair tied up in a ponytail. He wore a close-fitting black deepsuit and large diving boots.

"So, you got on the wrong side of the Professor too, did you?" said the stranger.

"You could say that," Lia said.

"What did you do?" Max asked. He glanced at the eye patch. "Are you – a pirate?"

The man groaned. "No! Everyone thinks I'm a pirate just because I've got an eye patch. I happen to have an eye infection, that's all. Anyway, aren't you going to introduce yourselves?"

"I'm Max – and these are my friends, Lia and Ko."

The man grunted. He glanced briefly at Lia but didn't look at Ko at all. "I'm Roger."

Max nearly said "Jolly Roger?" but stopped himself in time. Roger didn't look as if he'd be amused. "So – what did you do to anger the Professor?" Max asked.

"Oh – this and that," Roger said mysteriously. "I've been locked up for days. Now you're here, perhaps we can come up with an escape plan. With three of us on the case—"

"Four," Max said, pointing at Ko.

"Him?" Roger said. "I didn't count the Sea Ghost. They're useless, spineless creatures."

I don't like Roger, Ko's voice said in Max's head.

"I don't think I do, either," Max said aloud.

"What?" Roger said.

"Oh – nothing," Max replied.

"We need to concentrate on how to get out of here," Lia said. "We don't have any tools, the Spider Bots took away Max's hyperblade—"

"Wait," Max said. "I do have something." He took out the rocketball.

Roger took the ball from Max and squinted at it. "What use is this?" he said. "It's just a kid's toy."

"Don't be so sure," Max said. "Do the Spider Bot guards patrol past this cell?"

"Every now and again," Roger said. "What are you going to do, bounce a ball at them?"

"Not exactly," Max said. "If I can just boost the power…" He looked around the cell. It had lights so there had to be a power supply somewhere. He saw a metal plaque set into the grille. He tried to prise it off with his fingernails but the panel didn't budge. "Ow!" Max said, rubbing at his hands.

Let me try, said Ko's voice.

Ko went over to the panel and flattened his fingers out until they were wafer-thin. He slid them into the gap between the panel and the grille, and pulled. At last, the plaque came away and clattered onto the floor.

"Nice work, Ko!" Max said. The Sea Ghost smiled at him.

Below the panel was a tangle of wires. Max pulled out two of them, opened up the rocketball and spliced the wires onto the ball's circuitry. The lights in the cell flickered and dimmed.

"Impressive," said Roger. "But what, exactly, does it do?"

Max didn't answer. "That should do it. It's supercharged!"

Lia was by the cell door. "One of the guards is coming!" she said.

Max heard the clattering tread of a Spider Bot approaching. Quietly, he moved to the front of the cell.

As the Spider Bot passed, Max whistled. The Spider Bot turned its round, metal head, flashing its red eyes at Max.

He drew back his arm and hurled the rocketball as hard as he could.

Clang!

The supercharged rocketball hit the Spider Bot's head like a guided missile. The Spider Bot staggered, and sparks fizzed as the red

lights of its eyes went out. It collapsed to the floor in a tangle of legs.

"Quick!" Max said. "Before someone comes!" He put his arm through the bars, trying to grab hold of the Spider Bot, but no matter how much he strained it remained just out of reach.

"Leave it to me," Roger said. He stretched one arm through the bars and caught hold of a Spider Bot leg. The veins on his forehead bulged as he dragged the heavy robot towards the cell. When it was close enough, Max and Lia reached through the bars to help.

"What would you do without me, eh, messmates?" Roger said.

Lia glanced at him suspiciously. "I thought you said you weren't a pirate," she said.

Max wanted to remind Roger that without Ko's help they'd never have been able to knock out the guard in the first place. But he had a feeling Roger wouldn't listen.

Lia plucked the key card from the tip of the Spider Bot's leg. She inserted it into the slot beside the door.

With a smooth electronic whirr, the door slid open.

Max punched the air. "Yes!"

Lia grinned. "Now all we need to do is get out of here," she said.

SPIDER ATTACK!

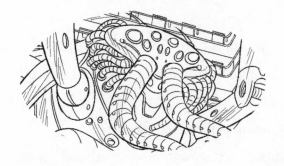

They made their way along the corridor, keeping to the shadows. Max and Lia moved as quietly as they could, and Ko was completely silent, but Roger's boots clanged on the walkway. Max winced at every footfall, hoping no Spider Bots were in earshot.

"We have to find Rivet and Spike," Max whispered. "Then we'll try to get through the energy web around the prison."

"Find who and who?" Roger asked.

"Rivet is my dogbot," Max explained.

"And Spike's my pet swordfish," Lia said. "I'm not leaving him here to be eaten!"

"My mother here too," Ko said. "We must find her."

Roger laughed. "Are you crazy? I'm not hanging round any longer than I need to, and I'm certainly not risking my neck for a robot dog, a fish and a Sea Ghost!"

Max heard a clattering up ahead. "Sshh!" he said. "Stop!"

They all froze. The clattering got nearer. Max recognised the noise – it was a Spider Bot on patrol.

"We have to hide!" Lia said. They were just passing a solid steel door. Lia produced the key card she'd taken from the Spider Bot guard, and inserted it in the slot. The door swung open.

They piled inside and Max quietly pulled

the door closed. Moments later they heard the Spider Bot go by.

"Whew!" Max said as the sound died away. "That was close. Let's get moving again."

"Wait," Ko said. "What all this stuff in here?"

Max blinked as his eyes got used to the dark. They were in a store room, with equipment stacked on shelves.

"Hey, look, here's my hyperblade!" He grabbed it from the shelf, and took a practice swipe, enjoying the hiss as it sliced through the air. "I feel a lot safer now I've got this back."

Roger took a blaster-gun. He aimed at an imaginary target, squinting down the barrel. "Powerbeam Blaster, Series Three. Nice." He tucked the blaster into his belt.

"If you've finished playing with all this technology stuff," Lia said, "we really need to get out of here."

They stepped out into the corridor and crept

onwards, senses on high alert. They'd hardly got halfway to the next door when Max heard the tread of another Spider Bot.

"Quick!" Max said, spotting a stairway off to the left. "Down here!"

They ran down the stairs just as the Spider Bot turned the corner – Max caught a glimpse of it, but he didn't think it had seen them.

At the bottom of the metal steps another walkway stretched out before them – the lowest floor. The walkway was only just above the water, which lapped around them on either side. Max saw an aquabuggy tied to a rail, bobbing in the water. It was a powerful-looking blue two-seater with a windscreen – almost twice the size of his own aquabike. *That could come in handy*, Max thought. Then, above the lapping of the water, he heard a familiar sound: Rivet's electronic bark.

"I'm coming, Riv!" he called. He ran along

the walkway, his boots clanking on the metal, in the direction of Rivet's bark. The others followed. Soon Max spotted his dogbot crouching in a cell.

Rivet jumped up on his hind legs, pawing at the cell bars. "Hello, Max!" he panted.

Spike was in a water-filled cell next to Rivet. He bumped against the glass, waving his fins, when he saw Lia.

Lia swiped the keycard in the slot by Rivet's cell. He scampered out, wagging his tail.

"Now, stand back, everyone," Lia said. She inserted the keycard for Spike. The glass wall of his cell rose and a cascade of water carried Spike over the walkway and into the sea.

Lia dived in after him, followed closely by Roger and Rivet.

They were in a narrow strip of water between the prison and the web of energy bars that surrounded it. *I wonder if I can cut through the bars with my hyperblade*, Max thought. There was only one way to find out.

He stood on the edge of the walkway, ready to plunge in. But just before he launched himself, he felt a tug on his sleeve. He turned to see Ko's round green eyes staring at him pleadingly. Max had almost forgotten about the Sea Ghost in the excitement of escaping.

"My mother in here," he said. "We find her, save her? Please?"

"Well..." Max said. He wanted to help. But it was only a matter of time before their escape was discovered and the alarm was raised.

"He's already betrayed us once!" Lia called up. "Why should we help him?"

Yes, he did betray us, Max thought, *but only because the Professor forced him to*. Max knew what it was like to lose your mother, as Ko had done. He made up his mind.

"All right, I'll help," he said to Ko. "But we

have to work fast." He turned to the others
bobbing in the water. "If we all look for Ko's
mother, we'll find her quicker."

"Yes, Max!" Rivet said. He paddled towards
the walkway.

"Oh, I suppose you're right," Lia grumbled.
But Roger just gave a sneering laugh.

"HARRR! No way am I going back up there for a scurvy Sea Ghost! I'm out of here!"

"Not so fast," Max said. "None of us can get out until we've neutralised the energy web."

"No problem!" Roger said. Treading water, he pointed his blaster at a control box mounted high on the wall. "I reckon if I hit that, all the systems will go down."

Max shook his head. "You can't do that. All the alarms will go off. Just wait, I can find a way to switch off the web without—"

"Waiting's for landlubbers!" Roger said. He squeezed the trigger. A bolt of orange light shot from the blaster and the control box exploded into smithereens.

There was a crackling, buzzing sound. The bright silver web that surrounded the prison flickered, dimmed and died.

"See?" said Roger. "Nothing to worry about."

The air was suddenly filled with the earsplitting wail of sirens.

"Oops. Well, so long, messmates!" Roger said. He pressed a button on his wrist and the glass visor of his deepsuit slid down over his face. He twisted in the water, and there was a roaring sound as twin jets fired out of his boots. With a kick, he dived out of sight.

Now what? Max thought, as the sirens blared. Should they stay and help look for Ko's mother, or get out while they still could?

"Oh, no!" Lia shouted. "Look!"

She pointed upwards. The huge figure of Shredder the Spider Droid, squatting on top of the prison, had stirred into life.

Its legs moved as if it was flexing its robotic muscles. Its round head stared down at them, the red eyes flashing.

Then Shredder crouched and sprang from the structure into the water.

Released from the spider's weight, the

whole prison rocked violently, and Max fell to his hands and knees. Waves crashed up onto the walkway, soaking Max and Ko, and the wailing of the siren cut out.

Max struggled to his feet as Shredder's body rose above the water. Its glaring red eyes fixed on Lia as it advanced towards her, swimming with surprising speed. Two of its giant legs chopped the water in front of it.

Without thinking, Max dived off the walkway. He pulled out his hyperblade and kicked out towards Shredder.

One of the spider's giant limbs loomed up in front of him. Max slashed at it. The hyperblade bit into the metal with a grinding clash.

Shredder stopped swimming and turned to look at Max. It towered over him, lifting four of its legs, and Max saw with horror that each one ended in a deadly hyperblade. They hung above him like executioners' swords.

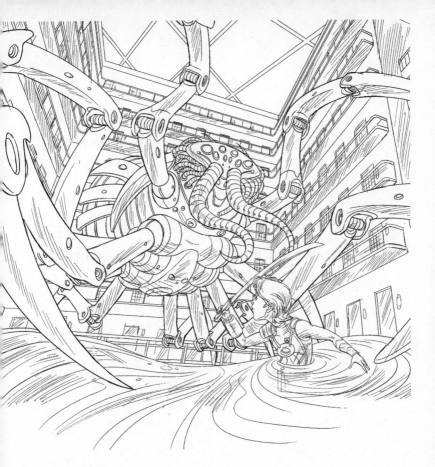

With a vicious swish, all four blades descended.

Max tumble-turned and dodged just as the blades whistled past. But the creature was still coming towards him, its hyperblades slicing at the water.

I see why it's called Shredder, Max thought.

CHAPTER EIGHT

FIRST BLOOD

The blades sliced at the water again, narrowly missing Max. He swam away as fast as he could, but the Robobeast kept advancing.

A blade swept towards him from the side.

Clang!

Max got his own hyperblade up just in time to parry the blow. The jolt ran right up his arm.

How could he defeat Shredder? It wasn't like the Robobeasts he'd faced before. Those had been real live creatures with a robotic control harnessed to them. Once he'd disabled the control, they'd returned to their natural state. But Shredder's natural state was killer robot.

If I don't do something fast, he thought, *I'll be slashed to ribbons.*

He dived under the water, hoping Shredder couldn't reach him down there.

Wrong.

Two of Shredder's legs plunged down towards him. Max twisted away from one. The other slashed across his chest. The hyperblade was so fine and sharp that Max felt almost no pain. But he saw his suit split wide open, and a ribbon of blood curl out into the water.

Max felt a powerful current push against him. Shredder was diving down to get him, its vast bulk displacing the water. He saw its red eyes gleaming, and all four of its front hyperblades sliced at him. He squirmed out of the way, shooting back up to the surface.

"Are you all right?" Lia was suddenly beside him, sitting astride Spike with the Amphibio mask still covering her face. "You're bleeding!"

Max touched his chest. His fingers came away covered in blood. "It looks bad, but it's just a scratch," he said, hoping that was true.

Next time, though, he might not be so lucky. Max couldn't dodge Shredder forever. But how could he strike back? His hyperblade didn't seem to be doing much damage.

"Look out!" Lia said.

The enormous sea spider surfaced with a crash, making waves as water poured off its back. It made straight for Max and Lia, legs chopping the water like scythes.

Max was about to kick away when Shredder

slowed down. Its eyes swivelled from Max to Lia and back again. *As if it's working out which one of us to get first*, Max thought.

"I save you!" said a voice from behind them. Max turned just in time to see Ko dive off the walkway. He shot forward like

a torpedo and crashed into Shredder's body, beating at the sea spider with his fists.

"No," Max yelled. "Ko! It's too dangerous!"

Shredder gave an electronic hiss which chilled Max's blood. It turned away from him and Lia, trying to locate this new threat. *Maybe it can only hunt down one enemy at a time*, Max thought.

The sea spider's legs scrabbled wildly, the blades just missing Ko.

"Get away from there, Ko!" Lia shouted. "Swim for it!"

Ko pushed off from the robot creature's side and streaked away through the water, leaving a white wake behind. Max had never seen him swim so fast.

"Wow!" Max said. "Those Sea Ghosts can really swim!"

Lia looked a little annoyed. "So can Merryn!" she said.

Shredder made a grinding noise, like an engine moving up through its gears, and gave chase. All eight legs churned up the water behind it. Max's relief ebbed away. Even Ko wouldn't be fast enough to stay ahead for long.

"Come on!" Max said. "We have to help!"

Lia didn't argue. She and Spike swam after the sea spider at top speed. Max and Rivet followed as fast as they were able.

Ko doubled back, heading for the Crystal Column. The sea spider turned slowly, and Ko widened the distance between them. But soon Shredder was churning through the water again, gaining on the Sea Ghost. Lia and Spike followed as fast as they could, but couldn't catch up.

Rivet struck out with a burst of speed and launched himself at Shredder.

Clang!

The dogbot smashed into Shredder's side and bounced off. But this time, the spider did not react and turn on its attacker as it had done with Ko.

That's strange, Max thought. *Maybe it's only programmed to attack living things, not robots like Rivet...* That made sense – otherwise it might have attacked the Spider Bot guards at the prison.

Ko swam straight at the Crystal Column, but swerved at the last moment. Shredder couldn't change course so quickly. It tried to slow down, engine grinding, legs beating at the water – then hit the Crystal Column with a crash that seemed to fill the whole cavern. Pieces of crystal flew off and splashed in the water. Shredder fell back into the sea in a tangle of waving legs.

Smart move, Ko! thought Max.

But the sea spider righted itself at once.

It flipped upright, and the water poured off its shining, undamaged surface. Max's heart sank. *If an impact like that doesn't damage it,* he thought, *what will?*

Shredder started to chase Ko around the Crystal Column. It was only a matter of time before it caught him – Ko was slowing down now, already growing tired.

Max looked at the column and an idea flashed into his mind. "Lia!" he shouted. "Can you help Ko? I've got a plan!"

"Right," Lia said. "Now we'll see who's faster – Merryn or Sea Ghost!"

"Here, boy!" Max said to Rivet.

The dogbot paddled over, looking none the worse for his encounter with Shredder. "Yes, Max?"

"I need to reprogramme you."

"Yes, Max," said Rivet.

They clambered out of the sea, back onto

the prison walkway. Max opened Rivet's control panel. He began to close down the power circuits controlling Rivet's speech, the glowing of his eyes and the wagging of his tail. Then he redirected all the power to Rivet's jaws.

Max looked up to see that Lia and Spike had almost caught up with Shredder. But it was too late. The Spider Droid had Ko cornered against the column, trapped between its two front legs. A third leg rose above its head...

Lia skimmed through the sea spider's legs and grabbed Ko's arm. Just seconds before the Robobeast could slam the hyperblade down, she pulled Ko away and onto Spike's back. Shredder's blow descended on empty water, sending up a splash of spray.

"Stay close to the column!" Max called out.

Spike ducked under Shredder's legs and then resurfaced, swimming fast around the

Crystal Column with Lia and Ko on his back.

Max snapped Rivet's control panel shut. "Follow me!" he said.

They plunged back into the water, and struck out for the Crystal Column, as far away from Shredder as possible. Max was relieved to see that up close the surface was full of hollows and handholds. He dug his fingers into a crack and hauled himself, dripping, out of the water. Rivet scrambled up behind him, using his jaws to hold on. Max climbed as fast as he could, hoping that Lia was managing to fend the Spider Droid off below.

"This is high enough," Max said, once they were a good distance above the Robobeast. "Get to work, Rivet – chew out a big chunk of that crystal!"

It was strange not to hear Rivet reply "Yes, Max," but still, the dogbot got right to work.

Rivet's iron jaws bit into the crystal with a grinding noise. Glittering shards flew off. Max helped, using his hyperblade to dig into the outline Rivet was making.

"What are you doing?" Lia's voice floated up from the water below. She and Ko were still riding on Spike, who was darting around the column, only just out of reach of Shredder's hyperblades. Max could see from his slowing speed that Spike was losing steam.

"Get the spider over here!" Max shouted.

Rivet had dug around a multi-coloured chunk of crystal bigger than Max's head, and it was dangling loose. Max wouldn't want to be underneath it when it fell.

"Come and get us, Shredder!" Lia shouted. Spike came in close to the column, with the giant spider just behind. *Any minute now*, thought Max. As soon as the Spider Droid was directly underneath, Spike dived below the water, taking Lia and Ko with him.

With all his strength, Max thrust his hyperblade at the last piece that held the crystal chunk in place. He felt it give, and with a thundering sound it tumbled down the column. *Smash!*

"Yes!" he shouted, as the crystal landed

right on Shredder's head.

There was an electronic squeal and two of the spider's eyes went dark.

It hissed angrily and rose up from the water, stretching its legs towards Max.

Max couldn't believe it – the rock hadn't been big enough! And now, slowly, Shredder began to clamber up the Crystal Column towards Max.

"Rivet!" Max shouted. "Go higher. We need an even bigger piece – much bigger! As fast as you can!"

The dogbot's iron paws dug into the rock as it clambered up the column and got to work again with its metal jaws.

Now all I have to do is hold off that Spider Droid, thought Max. *Easier said than done.* Holding on tight to a ledge in the crystal with one hand, he brandished his hyperblade with the other.

As the first of Shredder's legs probed its way towards him, he struck at it. His solid vernium blade bit deep into the Robobeast's limb. Shredder hissed and yanked back its leg. Max didn't know if the creature could feel pain. Perhaps it was just programmed to avoid damage. But another leg was already arcing towards Max. He swung out of the way and swiped again with his hyperblade. Again, the leg withdrew.

The sea spider hauled itself closer, its metal parts whirring as it moved. Its six remaining eyes glowed with menace.

Clinging onto the ledge, Max felt as if his arm was being pulled out of its socket. Plus, his chest hurt from where the Spider Droid had wounded him. Now that the shock had worn off, every breath was painful.

He struck again, and another one of Shredder's eyes fizzed out.

The Robobeast hissed.

It inched further up, holding onto the rock with four legs. The other four slowly encircled Max. He couldn't beat them all back.

"Max!" shouted Lia. "Look out! Above you!"

Max glanced up and saw that Rivet had managed to loosen an immense crystal boulder. As he watched, it broke free and thundered down the side of the column...

Straight at his head.

CHAPTER NINE

JAILBREAK

Max saw the massive chunk of crystal fall towards him, as if in slow motion.

He flattened himself against the side of the column. No, it would still crush him...

"Jump!" shouted Lia from below.

But Max felt frozen to the spot. At the last instant, he managed to push away from the column and dive.

The crystal boulder was so close, it scraped his heels as it fell.

Twisting in mid-air, Max saw the rock

hit Shredder just where its head and body joined. There was an almighty *CRACK* and the Robobeast's head snapped clean off. Shredder's body tumbled down to the sea, and hit the water with a huge splash at the same time as Max.

Underwater, Max saw the broken body of Shredder drifting down towards the ocean bed, its legs twitching.

With powerful strokes, Max swam back up to the surface.

"Well done, Riv!" he shouted. "You did it!"

Rivet couldn't answer without his voice, but he scrambled back down the Crystal Column and jumped into the sea to join Max.

There was a splash nearby as Lia and Ko broke the surface on Spike's back.

"Phew!" Lia said. "Well done, Max! Now, can we get out of here?"

"We still have to look for Ko's mother," Max reminded her.

Lia nodded. "All right. And while we're at it, let's get all the prisoners out."

They swam back to the prison and climbed onto the walkway, leaving Spike in the sea. Max opened Rivet's control panel and quickly restored his normal functions.

Rivet's tail wagged. "Got the big spider, Max," he said proudly.

"Look out!" Ko shouted.

A Spider Bot was scuttling along the walkway towards them, carrying a blaster in its front legs.

Max leaped to his feet, ran at the Spider Bot and brought his hyperblade slicing down on its head.

The Spider Bot made a fizzing noise, collapsed in a heap and lay still.

Lia prised the blaster from the Bot's limbs. "This might come in useful."

"There must be a control centre where we can override the security system," Max said. "It'll be quicker than unlocking every cell one by one."

They ran along the corridors, making their way to the centre of the prison.

Two Spider Bots ran out from a doorway. "Intruder alert!" one said. The other raised its blaster rifle.

Lia fired off two shots with her own blaster, and the Spider Bots fell in smoking, blackened heaps.

"You're getting used to technology, aren't you?" Max said. Lia grinned under her mask.

"Here!" Ko said, pointing to the room the Spider Bots had come from. "Is this control centre?"

Max led the way into the room. There were banks of video monitors around the wall, showing all the cells, and a console with controls for the prison systems. He found the Command menu and scrolled down until he found an option that said OVERRIDE ALL LOCKING SYSTEMS. Max selected it.

Immediately, clanging noises came from all over the prison.

On the monitor screens, all the cell doors swung open. The prisoners looked around, stunned, and then began to stream out – humans, Merryn, Kroy, and all kinds

of other creatures. Max could soon hear their movements and excited voices on the walkways outside.

But Ko looked disappointed. "I not see my mother," he said. "I go look."

They made their way back to the walkway at the edge of the floating prison. All the freed prisoners were diving back into the sea, shouting and whooping for joy. There were one or two Sea Ghosts among them. Ko approached them and they stood as if in conversation, but saying nothing. Max guessed they were speaking in each other's heads. Ko looked worried.

"She's not here?" Max called.

"They not know," Ko replied. "Not see her."

"Let's go back and look for her," Lia said.

They ran to check the cells. The prison was quiet and their footsteps echoed. Every cell they looked into was empty – until, at last, Max saw the pale figure of a Sea Ghost woman crouched in a dark corner. She looked at him with big green eyes but didn't move. Max's heart flooded with relief.

"Ko!" he called. "I think I've found her!"

Ko came in. He ran to the Sea Ghost woman and hugged her. The woman hugged him back, but feebly. They clung to each other, and Max guessed that they were speaking in the Sea Ghost language.

Lia came in. "Oh, good, we found her!"

"Is my mother, Allis," Ko said. "But she sick. Need healer. In my home city. Can you help?"

"Of course," Max said. He looked at Lia, expecting her to argue, but she caught his eye and nodded. *I guess she's coming around to Ko*, he thought. Then he remembered the aquabuggy he'd seen tied up under the walkway. "We'll get her home."

Max and Ko carried Allis to the walkway

outside, where Spike was waiting for them. Allis weighed almost nothing, but her skin felt hot and shivery. *She must have some kind of fever*, Max thought.

They carefully set Ko's mother down in the aquabuggy. At once she sank back in the passenger seat, and her eyes closed. Max slid into the driver's seat and Rivet scrambled up onto the back.

"I'll ride on Spike," Lia said to Ko. "If you get tired of swimming, you can ride too."

The Sea Ghost nodded. "Thank you," he said.

Max hit the starter button and the aquabuggy roared into life. He steered away from the prison and rounded the Crystal Column, enjoying the power and speed of his new vehicle.

A glimmer caught Max's eye. Looking up, he saw something sticking out of the side of the column – the tip of one of Shredder's legs. *It must have snapped off when the crystal boulder hit it!* he thought.

"Wait," Max said. He brought the aquabuggy to a halt next to the Crystal Column and leaped across to it. Then he began to climb.

"What are you doing?" Lia called.

"I'm not leaving a bit of kit like that behind," Max said. "You never know when it might come in handy."

He tugged and tugged until the metal shard came out of the column. It was as long as one of his own legs and ended in a curved hyperblade, even sharper than his own. He was lucky it had only scratched him in the fight. Carefully, he climbed down and strapped it to the back of his aquabuggy.

"Ready?" he said. "Which way?"

Ko pointed straight ahead.

Max revved the engine and put his foot on

the accelerator. The aquabuggy roared across
the smooth, dark sea. Spike leaped alongside
with Lia on his back. Then the swordfish dived
beneath the water, and Max and Ko followed.

He saw Lia pull her Amphibio mask off and suck water into her gills.

We said we'd help Ko's people, Max thought, *and that's what we're doing. We have to stop the Professor destroying this world, and Sumara too.*

He wondered if there would be any more deadly Robobeasts to face along the way...

Knowing the Professor, Max had a feeling there would be.

Don't miss Max's next Sea Quest adventure,
when he faces

STINGER
THE SEA PHANTOM

Look out for all the books in
Sea Quest Series 3:

THE PRIDE OF BLACKHEART

TETRAX THE SWAMP CROCODILE
NEPHRO THE ICE LOBSTER
FINARIA THE SAVAGE SEA SNAKE
CHAKROL THE OCEAN HAMMER

OUT IN MARCH 2014!

WIN AN EXCLUSIVE GOODY BAG

In every Sea Quest book the Sea Quest logo is hidden in one of the pictures. Find the logos in books 5–8, make a note of which pages they appear on and go online to enter the competition at

www.seaquestbooks.co.uk

Each month we will put all of the correct entries into a draw and select one winner to receive a special Sea Quest goody bag.

You can also send your entry on a postcard to:

Sea Quest Competition, Orchard Books,
338 Euston Road, London, NW1 3BH

Don't forget to include your name and address!

GOOD LUCK

Closing Date: December 30th 2013

IF YOU LIKE SEA QUEST, YOU'LL LOVE **BEAST QUEST!**

Series 1: COLLECT THEM ALL!

An evil wizard has enchanted the magical beasts of Avantia. Only a true hero can free the beasts and save the land. Is Tom the hero Avantia has been waiting for?

978 1 84616 483 5

978 1 84616 482 8

978 1 84616 484 2

978 1 84616 486 6

978 1 84616 485 9

978 1 84616 487 3

DON'T MISS THE
BRAND NEW SERIES OF:

Series 14: THE CURSED DRAGON

978 1 40832 920 7

978 1 40832 921 4

978 1 40832 922 1

978 1 40832 923 8

OUT IN JANUARY 2014!